for Sylvia and Fraser
K.B.

CIP Data is available.
Published in the United States 1998 by Dutton Children's Books,
a member of Penguin Putnam Inc.
375 Hudson Street, New York, New York 10014
Originally published in Great Britain 1997 by Andersen Press Ltd., London
Typography by Richard Amari
Printed and bound in Italy by Grafiche AZ, Verona
First American Edition
ISBN 0-525-45952-9
2 4 6 8 10 9 7 5 3 1

The WOLF IS COMING!

by **Elizabeth MacDonald**
illustrated by **Ken Brown**

Dutton Children's Books ■ *New York*

A family of rabbits was nibbling dandelion leaves on the hillside when a wolf crept out of the forest and bounded toward them.

"The wolf is coming! The wolf is coming!" cried the father rabbit, thumping his foot on the ground to warn the others.

So the whole rabbit family ran down the hill and through the fields. And when they could run no more, they came to a little wooden coop, where a hen and her chicks lived.

"The wolf is coming! The wolf is coming!" cried the father rabbit. "Please let us hide in your coop, kind hen!"

"Come in, and welcome," clucked the hen, and they
all squeezed into the little wooden house together.
But just as the rabbits were getting their breath back, the
hen peeped out of her little house and saw the wolf coming.
"*Cluck-cluck-cluck!*" she screeched. "The wolf is coming!"

So the hen and her chicks and the whole rabbit family ran out of the coop and through the farmyard. And when they could run no more, they came to the pigsty where a mother pig and her piglets lived.

"The wolf is coming! The wolf is coming!" squawked the hen.

"Please let us hide in your sty, kind pig!"

"Come in, and welcome," grunted the mother pig, and they all squeezed into the sty together.

But just as they were beginning to feel safe, the mother pig peeked out of her sty and saw the wolf coming.

"*Oink-oink-oink!*" she squealed. "The wolf is coming!"

So the mother pig and her piglets, the hen and her chicks, and the whole rabbit family ran out of the sty and past the barn. And when they could run no more, they came to the cow shed, where a brown cow was looking after her two little calves.

"The wolf is coming! The wolf is coming!" squealed the mother pig. "Please let us hide in your shed, kind cow!"

"Come in, and welcome," mooed the brown cow, and they all squeezed into the cow shed together.

But before they had time to make themselves comfortable, the brown cow peered out of the cow shed and saw the wolf coming.

"*Moo-oo! Moo-oo!*" she cried. "The wolf is coming!"

So the brown cow and her calves, the mother pig and her piglets, the hen and her chicks, and the whole rabbit family all ran out of the cow shed and down the lane. And when they could run no more, they came to a rickety old shack where the gray donkey lived.

"The wolf is coming! The wolf is coming!" mooed the brown cow. "Please let us hide in your shack, kind donkey!"

"Oh well, if you must," said the donkey, "but I'm not scared of a silly old wolf!"

All the animals scrambled to get through the door at the same time, making a frightful noise. There was thumping and clucking and cheeping and grunting and squealing and mooing until…

"QUIET!" brayed the donkey. "Hold your breath or we will never fit!"

At once the noise stopped. But the donkey had only just managed to get the door closed, when he saw the wolf creeping closer.

"The wolf is coming!" he brayed.

"The wolf is coming! The wolf is coming!" shrieked all the other animals.

As they all let their breath out at once, the rickety old shack burst apart. There was such a commotion as all the animals exploded onto the ground that the poor old wolf was frightened out of his wits.

As fast as his legs could carry him, he ran back across the meadow, past the cow shed, through the farmyard, and over the hill. And when he could run no more, there he stayed.

So the cow and her calves ambled back to the cow shed, the mother pig and her piglets hurried back to their sty, the hen and her chicks raced back to their coop, and the whole rabbit family went back to the hillside.

As for the donkey, he brayed as loud as he could until the farmer came to put his home back together again. And they all lived in peace for the rest of their lives.

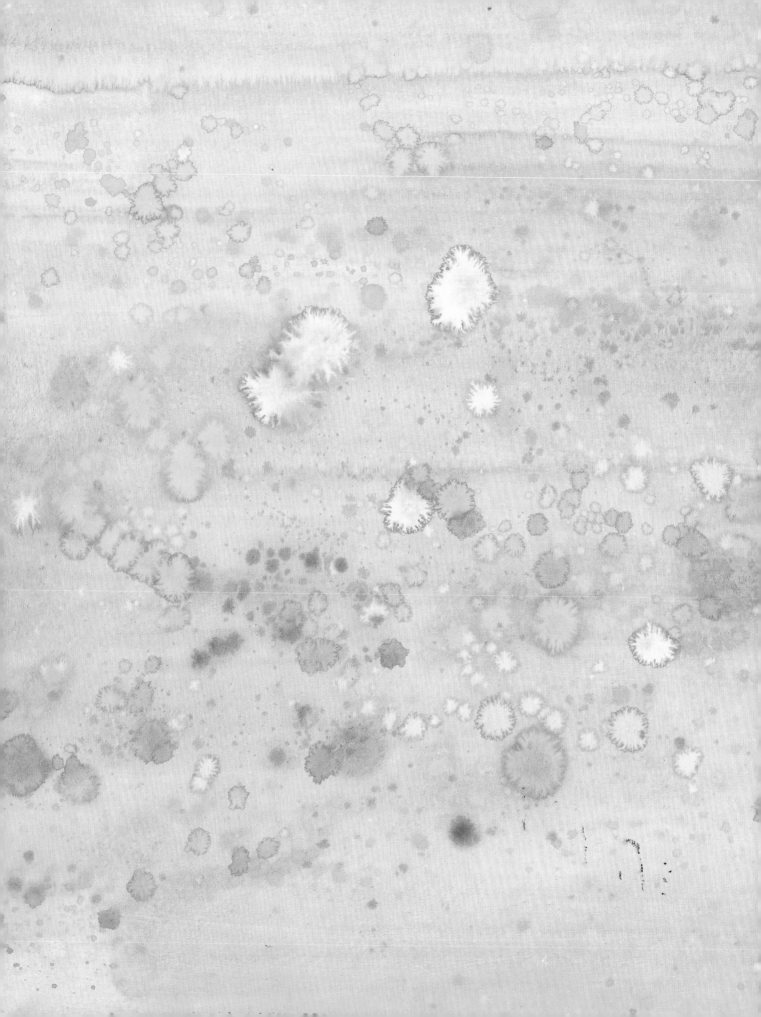